THE DRAGONSLAYERS

Professor Wacko Kilowatt stood with the bigwigs by his side. "We have," he pronounced, "in accordance with the facts and our unrivaled scientific knowledge come to a conclusion that Dippy is either a hoax or a figment of Jacob Two-Two's imagination."

"What's a figment of the imagination?" Jacob Two-Two asked.

"I mean, and I'm speaking scientifically, you little squirt, that you made him up in your head and he doesn't really exist."

Suddenly Dippy raised his huge neck and began to roar. Teeth as large as bananas flashed in the sun. He opened his mouth wider and sent out his long wet pink tongue. Wacko and his helpers stumbled over each other, reeling backward.

"It's plain to see," Wacko hollered, "that this freak of nature, this beast ugly beyond compare, is a menace. I will advise the prime minister that he is to be exterminated. We will return with airplanes and use Dippy for target practice."

"Oh, no you won't," Jacob Two-Two said. "Oh, no you won't."

Jacob Two-Two and the Dinosaur

by Mordecai Richler

illustrated by Norman Eyolfson

A BANTAM SKYLARK BOOK®
TORONTO • NEW YORK • LONDON • SYDNEY • AUCKLAND

RL 5, 008-012

*This edition contains the complete
text of the original hardcover edition.*
NOT ONE WORD HAS BEEN OMITTED.

JACOB TWO-TWO AND THE DINOSAUR
*A Bantam Skylark Book / published by arrangement with
Alfred A. Knopf, Inc.*

PRINTING HISTORY
*Alfred A. Knopf edition published April 1987
Skylark Books is a registered trademark of Bantam Books. Registered in U.S. Patent and
Trademark Office and elsewhere.*

Bantam edition / May 1988

ISBN 0-553-15589-X

Published in the United States

Bantam Books are published by Bantam Books, a division of Bantam Doubleday Dell
Publishing Group, Inc. Its trademark, consisting of the words "Bantam Books" and the por-
trayal of a rooster, is Registered in U.S. Patent and Trademark Office and in other countries,
Marca Registrada. Bantam Books, 666 Fifth Avenue, New York, New York 10103

PRINTED IN THE UNITED STATES OF AMERICA

CW   0 9 8 7 6 5 4 3 2 1

For Daniel, Noah, Emma,
Marfa, and Jacob

As a child, I could imagine the world of dinosaurs. At times I was a dinosaur. And so rather than do something practical when I grew up, I just stayed with dinosaurs.

Dale A. Russell, of the Canadian National Museum of Natural Sciences, in Ottawa, as quoted in *The Riddle of the Dinosaur*, by John Noble Wilford

Jacob Two-Two
and the Dinosaur

1

When he was six years old, a mere child, he was known as Jacob Two-Two. He was given the name because he was two plus two plus two years old. He had two ears and two eyes and two feet and two shoes. He also had two older brothers, Daniel and Noah, and two older sisters, Emma and Marfa. But most of all, he was given the name because, as Jacob Two-Two himself once admitted, "I am the littlest in our family. Nobody hears what I say the first time. They only pay attention if I say things two times."

But now that he was eight years old he felt that he was too grown up to go by such a childish name. All the same, it stuck to him. After all, he still had two older brothers and two older sisters. And, as they were quick to point out, if he had once been two plus two plus two years old, he was now—come to think of it—only two times two times two years old. Not much of a difference, they said, but they really didn't understand.

Jacob Two-Two had learned a good deal since he had been a mere six years old. He could now dial a telephone number, do joined-up writing of a sort, and catch a ball, providing Noah wasn't aiming it bang at his head. True, his two older brothers and his two older sisters were still taller and much more capable than he was. And snootier than ever, it sometimes seemed to him.

Marfa, for instance, who was only four years older than Jacob Two-Two, no longer allowed him into the bathroom with her. "I know you're too young and stupid to understand," she said, "but it just isn't right for you to take a shower with me anymore."

Even so, some things were looking up. Jacob Two-Two could now cut a slice of bread that wasn't a foot thick on one end and thin as a sheet of paper on the other—unless Emma gave him a poke at just the right moment and then squealed, "Oh, Mummy, I don't want to make any trouble, but look what the baby of the family just did to the last loaf of bread in the house."

School was also a problem. A big problem.

When Jacob Two-Two had been a mere six years old, the family had lived in a big rambling old house on Kingston Hill in England. A year later his father had moved them all to Montreal, Canada, where he had come from in the first place. This was a great hardship for Jacob Two-Two, because the kids at his new school in Montreal poked fun at his British accent. The trouble-maker-in-chief was fat Freddy Jackson. He would gather together a bunch of the other kids and then corner Jacob Two-Two in the schoolyard. "Hey, Jacob," he'd say, "what does your father put in his car to make it run?"

"Petrol," Jacob Two-Two would reply. "Petrol." Be-

cause when he was nervous or excited he still said many things two times.

"That's what they call gasoline over in stinky old England," Freddy would explain, even as the other kids had begun to giggle. Then, turning to Jacob Two-Two again, he would ask, "And what are we standing on right now?"

"The grahs."

Soon enough, however, Jacob Two-Two learned to say "gasoline" when what he really meant was "petrol." Practicing in front of a mirror, he even taught himself to say "grass" instead of "grahs."

Unfortunately, everybody in the family picked on Jacob Two-Two too. If, for instance, he came home from school in a cheerful mood and called out, "Am I ever starved! What's for dinner?" Noah was bound to leap up, make a frightening face, and say "Dead cow."

Once he came home from school and asked his father for a measly dollar so that he could go to the movies on Saturday morning. Noah, as usual, had to put in his two cents. "You can't give the child a dollar just like that," he said. "It would be spoiling him." (But Noah wasn't all bad. He often allowed Jacob Two-Two to tag along with him on his newspaper route. In fact, he actually allowed Jacob Two-Two to deliver the newspaper himself to any house with a sign that warned BEWARE OF THE DOG.)

"Your brother has a point, Jacob. You will have to win the money by proving your intelligence. Now then, are you ready for a quiz?"

4

"Yes," Jacob Two-Two said. "Yes, I am!"

"Good. Now you will have to concentrate, because I can allow you only five seconds on the first impossibly difficult question. Ready?"

"Ready!"

"Okay. Here we go. For a big fifty cents tell me how long was the Seven Years War?"

"Seven years!"

"Excellent! Brilliant! Now, watch out for the next question because it is about the kings of France. Ready?"

"Yes."

"Good. Here it comes. For another fifty cents tell me what Louis came after Louis the Fourteenth?"

"Louis the Fifteenth."

"Wow! You're really flying today, kid. You have won a dollar," his father said, handing it over. "Now, are you a chicken-livered, trembling coward, or would you like to try another question—a really easy one—for one thousand dollars?"

"Yes! Yes! I'll try it."

"All right, then. Here it is. Jacob Two-Two, for one thousand dollars cash, tell me how you spell 'chrysanthemum.'"

Jacob Two-Two groaned. Why, he thought, was everybody in the house always teasing him? Everybody. One day, sure enough, it got him into trouble at school, but that was Daniel's fault, teasing again. Jacob Two-Two had been lying on the living-room carpet showing off that he was now old enough to have homework to do in his very own

5

assignment book. Looking up from the book, he asked, "Does anybody know what 'denote' means?"

Daniel told him what it meant, but Jacob Two-Two should have guessed that something was up, because no sooner did Daniel explain the word than Emma hid her face in a pillow. Noah burst out laughing. Marfa whispered, "Hey, Daniel, you shouldn't have said that. He's just dumb enough to repeat it at school."

Actually Jacob Two-Two hardly ever spoke up in class, because he was still ashamed of his British accent. This worried his schoolteacher, Miss Sour Pickle. First thing at school the next morning, Miss Pickle turned to Jacob Two-Two. "Jacob, would you please stand up and tell the rest of the class the meaning of the word 'denote.'"

"Yes, Miss Pickle." And, remembering what Daniel had taught him, Jacob Two-Two said, "Denote is what you write with de pencil and de paper."

Everybody in the class began to laugh, except for Miss Pickle. "Well, I never!" she said. "What cheekiness! How very, very rude! Jacob, you go stand in the corner at once, and after class is out this afternoon you will stay behind to wash all the blackboards."

When Jacob Two-Two finally got out of school late that afternoon, the other kids were waiting for him. But they hadn't stayed behind to tease him about his British accent. Instead they wanted to be friends. All of them. Even fat Freddy.

Jacob Two-Two was thrilled. Things were working out for him in Montreal at last. *Then it happened.* At the dinner table that night his father announced, "Mummy and I are going to Kenya for two weeks. On safari. But don't worry. Aunt Ida is coming to stay with you."

"Oh, no," Noah groaned.

"Not Aunt Ida," Marfa said.

"You forget that I'm seventeen now," Daniel said, insulted. "We don't need anybody to stay with us. I can look after the others."

Jacob Two-Two was too sad to say anything.

2

Her name was Aunt Ida, but as far as Jacob Two-Two and his two older brothers and two older sisters were concerned she was the perfectly horrid Aunt Good-For-You. Aunt Good-For-You was their father's older sister. She never visited the house without bringing the children a gift that was good for them. Say, a quart of her homemade carrot juice. Or a large box of alfalfa sprouts. Or five spools of dental floss. If she brought candy bars, they were sugar-free and made of pressed dates and granola. Before handing them over she would say how lucky they were and how the children of China or India would be grateful for something so good for them. Thank you, Jacob Two-Two would say, because his mother was watching him closely. Thank you, Aunt Ida. Yum, yum.

On birthdays Aunt Good-For-You usually came with books that would help the children choose a sensible career or improve their table manners or teach them to be very, very nice to everybody, including obvious stinkers.

Aunt Good-For-You, who had never married, had no

children of her own. She was thin and tall and wore her gray hair in a bun. She didn't drink beer or wine or whiskey, which was no good for you, or ever lie down on a sofa to daydream, which was even worse for you.

Immediately after Jacob Two-Two's parents flew off to Kenya, Aunt Good-For-You opened all the windows to clear the house of the foul smell of Daddy's cigars. Then she went on a tour of inspection. She took down Daniel's *Sports Illustrated* bathing beauty calendar, saying it was bad for him, and she did the same with Emma's poster of Robert Redford, saying it was no good for her. Noah was told he couldn't play his David Bowie records, which were bad for him, and Marfa was made to do without her red nail polish, which was no good for her. They weren't allowed to watch just about everything on TV, because it was too violent. Or read lying down, because it was bad for their eyes. Or eat standing up, because it was no good for their digestion. But the very first night in the house she did promise to read aloud to Jacob Two-Two before he went to sleep. Aunt Good-For-You had brought along the first volume of the *Britannica Junior Encyclopedia*. "Tonight," she said, "we will begin with the letter *A*."

The first Saturday afternoon, sensing unrest in the house, Aunt Good-For-You surprised them, announcing, "I'm willing to take you out tonight for a real treat. Any ideas?"

"Dracula and the Nose-Pickers are playing at the Palace tonight," Daniel said. "They're really great! They chop pianos to bits, whack each other over the head with guitars, and spray the crowd with hot pig's blood."

"Don't you think," Noah asked, "that in view of how violent city life has become it would be good for us to learn something about self-defense?"

"Well, I'm not sure about that," Aunt Good-For-You said.

"Why don't we take in the new kung fu movie at Cinema V," Noah asked, "if only for educational purposes?"

"I'm all for a hockey game," Emma said, but of course she intended to play for the Montreal Canadiens one day.

"Why don't we eat dinner at the Ritz," Marfa said, "really pigging it, and then sign Daddy's name to the bill?"

The last time they had been to the Ritz it was their father who had taken them there for Sunday brunch. As she had lined up at the buffet table for her fifth helping of dessert, Marfa had earned a very dirty look from the waiter. "It's not for me," she had said, fluttering her eyelashes. "It's for my kid brother. My poor parents. It's very embarrassing for them to take such greedy-guts to a real restaurant."

"What would you like to do, Jacob Two-Two?" Aunt Good-For-You asked.

Absolutely anything, Jacob thought, except listen to another page of the *Britannica Junior Encyclopedia*. "Oh, I don't know," he said.

"What we are going to do," Aunt Good-For-You said, "is dine at the Contented Vegetarian Snack Bar."

Oh, no, Jacob Two-Two thought. Not mocked hamburgers again.

"And then," Aunt Good-For-You said, "we are going to a lecture at the Museum of Fine Arts on 'The Life of the

Dinosaurs.' The lecture will be illustrated. Now, isn't that fun?"

Everybody groaned.

But to Jacob Two-Two's surprise the lecture was better than fun—it was fascinating.

Like him, he learned, dinosaurs had a reputation for being dimwitted. Even so, they had been lords of all life on earth for something like seventy million years. Their name came from Greek and meant "terrible lizards." In their time, dinosaurs had been gigantic creatures, the largest weighing eighty tons and measuring twenty-seven yards. They had disappeared from the face of the earth about sixty-five million years ago. Nobody knew why for sure. Maybe it was because of their tiny brains, or it could have been due to the fact that other creatures ate their eggs. It was also possible that they had all gotten sick at the same time. Or that there had been a shower of meteorites on earth, wiping them out. But even today their fossils could sometimes be found as far away as Tanzania, in Africa, or as near as the province of Alberta, in Canada. "Fossil" comes from the Latin *fossilis*, meaning "dug up."

Some of the dinosaurs had been carnivores, that is to say, eaters of the flesh of other animals. Others had been herbivores, or vegetarians, just like Aunt Good-For-You. The best-known of the giant dinosaurs were the *Diplodocus*, *Brontosaurus*, and *Brachiosaurus*. It was once thought that yet another breed of dinosaur, the *Stegosaurus*, had two brains: a little one in its head and a much larger one at the base of its spine. In 1912 this inspired a poem written by Bert L. Taylor, a columnist for the Chicago *Tribune*. It began:

> *Behold the mighty dinosaur,*
> *Famous in prehistoric lore.*
> *Not only for his power and strength*
> *But also for his intellectual length.*
> *You will observe by these remains*
> *The creature had two sets of brains—*
> *One in his head (the usual place),*
> *The other in his spinal base.*

3

It seemed like centuries, but actually only two weeks had passed when Jacob Two-Two's mother and father came home. Happily, they smelled of cigars and champagne and perfume and everything else that was wonderfully bad for you. They had come with gifts, of course. Gifts that weren't good for children. Real Kikuyu spears and shields for the boys. Tribal necklaces for the girls. Then, opening a cigar box, their father said, "There is also this."

And out of the cigar box popped what appeared to be a green lizard.

"Oh, no," Emma said, fleeing in one direction.

"How disgusting," Marfa said, fleeing in the other direction.

"I found him on the shores of Lake Begoria," their father said. "We were standing beneath a towering cliff, watching a furious steam jet, maybe twenty feet high. Suddenly the earth rumbled and shuddered, knocking us off our feet. The water jet from the underground stream

burbled and bubbled, rising another hundred feet, and out of it shot this curious creature, which landed right on my chest. I smuggled him through customs for you."

The lizard, or whatever it was, stood in the center of the living-room carpet, looking everybody over.

"Is he ever ugly," Daniel said.

"Let me take him to my biology class," Noah said. "I'll bet my teacher would just love to cut him up."

"Oh, no you don't," Jacob Two-Two said. "Oh, no you don't! I like him. I'm going to keep him for a pet."

Then, to everybody's amazement, the lizard—or whatever it was—raced across the carpet, climbed into Jacob Two-Two's lap, and sat there, his head dipping slightly to one side.

"I'm going to call him Dippy," Jacob Two-Two said. "I'm going to call him Dippy."

4

Dippy, nourished only on rubbish, grew even faster than asparagus. He slept on a pile of the latest newspapers at the foot of Jacob Two-Two's bed in their house in Montreal. Only two weeks after he had popped out of the cigar box, he was as big as a full-grown cocker spaniel. Two months later, lo and behold, he was as large as a horse. By that time school was out and the family had moved to a cottage on a nearby lake for the summer. This was very fortunate, indeed, because obviously Dippy could no longer sleep at the foot of Jacob Two-Two's bed. He was too big to even fit in the bedroom anymore and was still growing bigger at an incredible rate. So Dippy slept out in the woods. But every morning, when Jacob Two-Two awoke, there was Dippy by his bedroom window, waiting for him, his head dipping slightly to one side, wagging the green tail that grew longer and longer every day.

Dippy didn't look like anything anybody on the lake had ever seen before. He had an enormous green head, somewhat scaly, with big red eyes and a wet darting pink tongue as long as a yardstick. There were one hundred and two teeth in his mouth, most of them as high and sharp as the biggest nails you ever saw but gleaming white. His forelegs were very short, ending in scaly fingers with sharp claws. His hind legs were much thinner, far longer, and also ended in sharp claws. He had a huge humpy back, a fat belly, and a curling tail longer than everything else about him put together. Let's face it, if you weren't a personal friend, Dippy looked like something out of a horror movie. Jacob Two-Two thought he was beautiful.

Every morning after breakfast Dippy would bend his forelegs at the elbows and lay his enormous head on the grass so that Jacob could slither up his neck and make himself comfy on his back. Then off the two of them would go for a gallop. This was great fun as far as Jacob Two-Two and Dippy were concerned, but it was more than somewhat upsetting to the other people on the lake. One morning, for instance, a farmer out plowing his fields saw them galloping toward him. He leaped off his tractor and ran two miles to the village church, where he promptly fell onto his knees, praying. Late one evening as Mr. and Mrs. Sloshed were driving home from a cocktail party they saw—or thought they saw—Jacob Two-Two and Dippy bounding across a field. Mr. Sloshed promptly slammed on the brakes and turned to his wife, trembling. "Did you just see what I saw?" he asked.

"Certainly not," she lied, "because I'm not an old drunkard like you."

Right there and then Mr. Sloshed swore to give up drinking for life.

There were other incidents. People began to complain. And soon enough Jacob Two-Two's father invited him into the library for a man-to-man talk. "Jacob Two-Two, I realize that I'm the one who brought Dippy over from Africa in a cigar box in the first place. But at the time I honestly thought he was fully grown."

Dippy was now as fat as an elephant and as high as a giraffe.

"Now the phone never stops ringing. Everybody is complaining about our—our monster."

"Dippy is not a monster."

"Speaking for myself, I now have to spend two hours a day out in my station wagon collecting rubbish just to keep Dippy's stomach from rumbling, and he's still growing. What if we donated him to the local zoo and I got you a pony instead?"

"I don't want a pony. I've got Dippy and I love him."

Jacob Two-Two's parents sat up late that night talking about their problem. They decided to register Jacob Two-Two for daily swimming lessons at the Certified Snobs' Golf and Country Club, whose members all agreed among themselves that they were the finest people on the lake. In fact, if Snobbers, as they were known, ever argued about anything, it was only about which one of them had inherited the most money or whose family had discovered the lake first.

Jacob Two-Two's parents felt that if Jacob was separated

from Dippy every morning they might grow apart, and later it would be easier to separate them once and for all. What they hadn't counted on was that Dippy, left to mope by himself in the woods for two mornings, would follow Jacob Two-Two to the Certified Snobs' Club on the third morning. This happened to be a very special day for the Snobbers. Their club president, the celebrated Professor Wacko Kilowatt, was to be honored at a luncheon. But even as he was taking his place at the head table, all the people at the other tables began to scatter, the women screaming, the men jumping into the lake. All because Dippy had just come trotting past, heading for the swimming pool.

It was a disgrace. A scandal. And that night an outraged Professor Wacko Kilowatt summoned Jacob Two-Two's father to the club and presented him with a petition signed by all the Snobbers.

"Look here," Wacko said, "we are now, in spite of what hopelessly inferior people say, a very tolerant club. We have come to accept a few members who are black or Italian or Jewish or Greek, so long as they are also filthy rich. We even accept children for swimming classes whose parents," he added, looking hard at Jacob Two-Two's father, "were not intelligent enough to inherit money and actually work for a living. But we must draw the line somewhere. We will simply not accept any green monsters in our club. That beast must not trample our grass anymore."

"I will see to that," Jacob Two-Two's father promised.

"Of course you will. But, unfortunately, everybody on

the lake is frightened. There are rumors that that ugly monster is an invader from another planet. As you know, I am the most distinguished scientist in the country. That creature has not only aroused my anger, but also my curiosity. Tomorrow morning I intend to visit your modest cottage with my staff of experts to establish exactly who and what that slimy thing is. I will establish this scientifically, of course."

5

Professor Wacko Kilowatt happened to be the very brightest light in Prime Minister Perry Pleaser's think tank.

Let me explain.

A think tank is not quite the same as either a tropical fish tank or an army tank. A think tank is made up of a group of people who are paid to think hard and deep. Every president or prime minister has one. Even the prime minister of Canada.

The prime minister of Canada was the Right Honorable Perry Pleaser. On awakening each morning, Perry Pleaser, even before he brushed his teeth, would hug himself and kiss his reflection in the mirror. He wanted all the people to love him at least as much as he loved himself, which was proving very, very difficult.

Like presidents and prime ministers everywhere, Perry Pleaser seldom went anywhere without his yes people. He had three yes men and three yes women.

Yes people are highly recommended. Everybody deserves two, never mind six. It is the duty of yes people to say yes to everything you suggest, no matter how foolish. So when Perry Pleaser arrived at his office each morning and broke into his famous smile and sang out, "Don't you think I'm absolutely, totally, one hundred percent wonderful?"

Yes, would say the yes men, and the yes women would call out yes, too.

Professor Wacko Kilowatt had not been put in charge of Perry Pleaser's think tank because of his beautiful baby-blue eyes. He was, in fact, short and fat and ugly. He had been thrust into his high office because of a famous scientific survey he had run to establish important facts about Canada's climate.

"I wonder," Perry Pleaser had said one morning, "what kind of climate we can expect next year."

Yes, said the yes men, and yes, said the yes women.

"Good. Then get me the celebrated Professor Wacko Kilowatt out of Playpen University in Montreal. Give him fifty million dollars—no, make it a hundred—and tell him not to come back until he has the hard facts."

Yes, said the yes women, getting in first for once, and then yes, said the yes men.

Then the prime minister said, "Now watch this," and he went on to tie his shoelaces without help from anybody.

"Wow!"

"Did you see that?"

The yes women applauded and the yes men whistled and stamped their feet.

Professor Wacko Kilowatt immediately put two hundred scientists to work. They sent satellites into outer space and shoved deep probes into the ground. They traveled from coast to coast, studying animal and plant behavior. They took cloud and soil samples. Then, after they had collected ten tons of data, they fed it into a computer large enough to fill a hockey arena. Two months later Professor Wacko Kilowatt burst into Perry Pleaser's office. "I've got it," he said.

"Shoot," Perry Pleaser said.

"On balance, to the best of my knowledge, with all the information available to us at this point in time, taking one consideration with another, allowing for computer error, human folly, miracles, and unforeseen difficulties . . . *it seems likely that next year it will be colder in January than July.*"

"This man is a genius," Perry Pleaser said.

Yes, said the yes men, and yes, said the yes women, too.

"Professor Wacko Kilowatt, I hereby appoint you head of my think tank. You will also serve as my scientific troubleshooter."

6

Professor Wacko Kilowatt arrived at the cottage on the lake accompanied by three official paleontologists. They came in a truck packed with equipment to measure and test and x-ray and otherwise annoy Dippy.

Paleontology comes from three Greek words and means "the science of ancient being," and paleontologists are men and women who study the history of past life by fooling around with fossils, usually the petrified bones of animals who died millions and millions of years ago.

"Okay," Wacko said at once, "where is the thing?"

"He is not a thing," Jacob Two-Two said angrily. "He is my pet and his name is Dippy."

"Ha," Wacko said. "Lead us to it. Or *him*," he added, winking at the paleontologists.

Dippy happened to be taking a snooze in the sun, his green humped back heaving like a mountain with each breath and his snores resounding like thunder.

"Does he bite?" Wacko asked, retreating a step.

"Scared?" Jacob Two-Two asked.

"Certainly not, you little runt." Then Wacko turned to the three trembling paleontologists. "Go ahead, men. Get on with it. I'll just climb that tree and watch from there."

So they got out their equipment and extension ladders and began to crawl all over Dippy. Dippy, stirring awake, yawned. The paleontologists leaped off him and ran for their lives.

"Come back at once, you cowards," Wacko called out from his perch in the tree.

Grudgingly the paleontologists crept back toward Dippy. They measured his jaw. They peeked in his ears. They took his blood pressure. They listened to his heart. "If I didn't know any better," the first paleontologist said, "I'd say he was a dinosaur."

"He certainly looks like one," the second paleontologist said.

"And measures like one," the third said.

Wacko slid down the tree. He pulled his hair. He stamped his feet. "But he can't be a dinosaur, you idiots. There hasn't been one alive on earth for sixty-five million years, give or take a year or two."

Wacko and the three paleontologists conferred. They consulted books. They studied charts. They appealed to their computers. Finally, Wacko was ready to pronounce. "We have," he said, "in accordance with the facts and our unrivaled scientific knowledge, come to a conclusion that cannot be disputed. Dippy is either a hoax or a figment of Jacob Two-Two's imagination."

"What do you mean, a hoax?" Jacob Two-Two's father demanded.

"Well," Wacko said, "how do we know he's not a giant elephant wearing a Halloween costume?"

"What's a figment of the imagination?" Jacob Two-Two asked.

"I mean, and I'm speaking scientifically, you little squirt, that you made him up in your head and he doesn't really exist."

"But here he is," Jacob Two-Two said. "Here he is."

"Here he is, only if you are eight years old, maybe not doing so hot in the second grade, and have not had the advantage of my celebrated intelligence."

"Dippy is a dinosaur," Jacob Two-Two said, "a genuine *Diplodocus*."

"Which only goes to prove that you're just a bit dippy yourself, kiddo."

Suddenly Dippy raised his huge neck and began to roar. Teeth now as large as bananas flashed in the sun. He opened his mouth wider and sent out his long wet pink tongue. Wacko and his helpers stumbled over each other, reeling backward.

"It's plain to see," Wacko hollered, "that this freak of nature, this beast ugly beyond compare, is a menace. We'll have to make arrangements to remove him from here."

"But how can you remove a figment of my imagination?" Jacob Two-Two demanded.

Ignoring Jacob Two-Two, Wacko turned to his helpers. "I have decided that he isn't a figment after all, but a hoax. A fraud. A vile attempt to trick honest scientists. I will advise the prime minister that he is to be exterminated. We

29

will return with airplanes and use Dippy for target practice. Why, we'll bomb the beast into oblivion."

"Oh, no you won't," Jacob Two-Two said. "Oh, no you won't."

7

After breakfast Dippy seemed depressed, very depressed, so he and Jacob Two-Two didn't set off on their usual gallop. Instead they sat down together in a clearing, Dippy lowering his head to the grass so that it was just at Jacob Two-Two's height.

"The professor's nutty as a fruitcake," Dippy said. "I am so a dinosaur. Not a hoax. Not a figment of your imagination. But a *Diplodocus*, just like you said."

"Dippy, you can talk! You can talk!"

"Of course I can talk, but you mustn't reveal that to anybody else. Or next thing I know they'll expect me to go to school or get a job." Dippy shed a huge tear. "Today is my birthday."

"Many happy returns. How old are you, Dippy?"

"Sixty-five million two hundred thousand and two hundred and twenty-two years old. I can talk and I can read, but I can't write."

"Oh, my, aren't you ashamed? I mean, at your age?"

"Please, don't *you* start criticizing me," Dippy said,

shedding another tear. "You're the only friend I've got in the whole wide world."

Jacob Two-Two hugged Dippy and kissed him on the cheek.

"How could I be expected to hold a pen or a pencil in these ridiculous hands?" Dippy said, raising an enormous claw.

"I see what you mean."

"No, you don't. The truth is, I'm an airhead. A real bubble-brain."

"Me too," Jacob Two-Two sang out. "Me too."

"That's why my species has been extinct for sixty-five million years, so far as I know."

"Everything's going to be okay, Dippy."

"No, it won't. I wish I were still frozen in that block of ice."

Dippy explained that he had been a mere babe when that slight earthquake in Kenya had dislodged him from his sixty-five-million-year-old prison, shooting him up from far below the surface of the earth, through the steam jet, right onto the chest of Jacob Two-Two's father.

"My good luck," Jacob Two-Two said.

"But possibly not mine. This is the wrong age for me, Jacob. The way I see it, the future is in computers and I can't even hold a pencil. Professor Kilowatt is right. I'm a freak of nature. Ugly beyond compare."

"No, you're not, Dippy. No, you're not. In fact, I think you're handsome."

"Do you think they're going to use me for target practice, Jacob?"

"Not so long as I'm here they won't."

"I'm willing to put my shoulder to the wheel, but who would hire me? In order to even apply for a job as a messenger boy I could no longer gallop about stark naked. I'd have to buy a suit and tie. Gosh, Jacob, do you know what that would cost? I mean, it would take hundreds of yards of material. I'll bet they couldn't find anything to fit me even in the outsize shop."

Dippy began to sob again. It was amazing. Jacob Two-Two had heard the expression "weeping buckets," but he had never actually seen it before.

"And I'm always hungry," Dippy moaned. "I'm just not getting enough to eat."

"But Dippy, my father brought you two station wagons full of rubbish only yesterday."

"I know, I know. I don't blame him. Having me around must be very difficult for him. I think it would be best for everybody if I just ran away."

"Oh, no, Dippy. Please don't. Please don't."

"I like you, Jacob. I think you're terrific." Dippy blushed a darker green. "But sometimes I wish I had a girlfriend."

"Aw, who needs girls," Jacob Two-Two said, irritated.

"It's okay for you to talk—you're only eight. But I'll bet when you get to be sixty-five million-plus years you'll be interested in girls too."

"It's no use brooding about it, Dippy. You're the only dinosaur left on the planet."

"Maybe yes and maybe no."

"What do you mean"

34

"One day when everybody in the house was out and I was still small enough to slip through the door, I sneaked into your father's library. I found a picture book about Canada, and there were all those high, high mountains. If there are any of us left I figure that's where they'd be hiding out."

"Oh, you mean the Rockies out in B.C.," Jacob Two-Two said.

"B.C. Right, right!" Dippy began to beat the earth with his forelegs. "B.C. is where I come from and B.C. is where I'm a-heading for. Yippee for B.C.!"

"Dippy, you're getting things mixed up. I know that in other countries B.C. stands for the years before Christ, but in Canada it stands for the province of British Columbia, which isn't quite the same thing."

"It's a good sign, though, isn't it? B.C., B.C. If there are any of us left, that's where they'll be."

"Please stay here with me, Dippy."

"I'd like to, Jacob, honestly. But if I am the last of my species it just wouldn't do for me to sit still and wait to be blown to oblivion."

"What are we going to do, Dippy?"

"Don't ask me. I'm a pea-brain. Thinking is your department."

"Don't worry," Jacob Two-Two said without conviction. "I'll come up with something."

8

Even as the two friends were deliberating, events beyond their control were already taking shape in Perry Pleaser's office in Ottawa. The prime minister wasn't feeling too hot. He had just returned from a disastrous national meet-the-people tour. Out there in Vancouver, he had plunged into a crowd in a shopping mall, saying, as was his habit, "Would anybody like my autograph? Or possibly some of you would like to kiss my hand? Go ahead. I don't mind." But when the people stepped forward it was to throw rotten eggs at him.

They pelted him with tomatoes in beautiful downtown Edmonton. They hissed him in Toronto. They heckled him in Montreal, where a man stood up and shouted, "If you're so clever, Perry Pleaser, tell us how long was the Seven Years War?"

"I do not respond to trick questions."

The people hooted. They howled. Perry Pleaser retreated to Ottawa and summoned Professor Wacko

Kilowatt to his office. "Wacko, what am I paying you for? Tell me how to restore my popularity."

"By doing something heroic," Wacko said.

"Like what?"

"What made Saint George such a hero?"

"He slayed a dragon."

"Right."

"But there aren't any more dragons."

"I just happen to know where one can be found."

"And you want *me* to slay it? *Wacko, what if I got hurt?*"

"There will be no risk to your person."

"In that case," Perry Pleaser said, leaping onto his desk top, "lead me to him. I'll pulverize him! Wait! Are you sure I can't get hurt, Wacko?"

"Absolutely."

"And am I really going to be a hero, Wacko?"

"Yes."

"Then let's not waste another minute. To arms, to arms! Lead me to that dragon!"

9

Jacob Two-Two once asked his father why he belonged to a glee club. "Well," his father said, "if I'm out of town, in a hotel, and you're not there, nor Mummy nor Daniel nor Noah nor Emma nor Marfa, it helps me to sing. You ought to try it, too, Jacob Two-Two, if ever you're feeling lonely and blue."

The glee club that Jacob Two-Two's father belonged to met once a month to gather around a piano and drink beer and sing the good old stuff: "My Darling Clementine"; "Down by the Old Mill Stream"; "A Bicycle Built for Two"; "Home on the Range." Songs like that. Once every summer they also got together at the cottage by the lake for the Annual Glee Club Big-Time Poker Game. This time out Jacob Two-Two's father won everybody else's money. In fact, he won $742 and went to bed very happy.

When Jacob Two-Two's father awoke the next morning, however, the money was gone. That wasn't very serious. But Jacob Two-Two was also gone. And that was very, very serious indeed.

Jacob Two-Two left a note. It read:

Dere Mumy and Dady,

   Dippy will not be used for targit practiz. I'm
taking him wher he wil be safe. Do not wory. I
will be back in time to begin schul.

Sincerely yurz,
Jacob Two-Two

P.S. Dady, I.O.U. 742 dollirs,
less one weke's allowince,
2 dollirs.

"Oh, my God," Jacob Two-Two's mother said. "What
will we do?"

Marfa had already begun to cry. So had Emma. Daniel
and Noah turned pale. And even as the family stood there,
grieving, the cottage filled with an incredible noise. It
shook and shuddered. Something was happening outside.
Everyone ran out to look.

"*Freeze, everybody!*" a voice called through a loud-
speaker. "*Hands up! We suffer from itchy trigger fingers. Har,
har, har!*"

A helicopter was whirring overhead. A mini-submarine
surfaced on the lake, its missile launcher pointed right at
the cottage. There were tanks everywhere. The cottage
was surrounded by soldiers carrying submachine guns.
"Is it safe now?" a trembly little voice asked.

"Yes, Mr. Prime Minister, it's quite safe."

So Perry Pleaser squirted forward. "In the name of the people of Canada, I demand that you surrender your dragon to me at once."

"It's not a dragon," Jacob Two-Two's mother said.

"It's a *Diplodocus*," Jacob Two-Two's father said.

"His name is Dippy," Marfa said.

"And he's not here," Emma said. "He ran away with Jacob Two-Two."

The family was held prisoner and then a search was made to establish what Jacob Two-Two had taken with him. The following items were discovered to be missing:

6 cans salmon
6 cans tuna
1 can opener
1 loaf sliced rye bread
1 pound homemade chopped chicken livers
1 box brownies
Various items of clothing
1 glee club songbook, in case he was feeling blue
1 flashlight
1 Swiss Army knife
1 frying pan
Noah's nylon tent, sleeping bag, and backpack
1 map of Canada

The army intelligence group pondered the list, scratching their heads. Finally one of them said, "Looks like the little fella was planning to set out on a trip."

"Good thinking, Bailey, but where to?"

The intelligence officers studied the list again. "Possibly, just possibly, somewhere in Canada," Bailey said.

"What makes you think that?"

"Well," he said, "after you've been in intelligence for twenty years, you get to trust your hunches."

Now the feared Bulldog Burke, chief of army intelligence, was brought in to question Jacob Two-Two's father. "We're going to start him right in on the infamous Smoked Meat Torture. Known as the Salt Beef Buster in England and the Pastrami Punch in the United States."

The other officers turned pale, filled with pity. But it was too late. The squad car that had been dispatched earlier to one of Montreal's finest delicatessens had already returned with the cruel instruments of torture.

It was, by this time, long past the lunch hour for poor Jacob Two-Two's father. His stomach was rumbling as he was tied into a chair and set down before the kitchen table, where he was joined by Bulldog Burke and his staff. Then the goodies were brought in, all of them placed just out of reach of Jacob Two-Two's father. A steaming platter of juicy, tender smoked meat, its wonderful aroma maddening to men, women, and children everywhere. Heaps of crisp French fried potatoes. Pickles. Hot dogs. Rye bread. Everybody dug in, except for Jacob Two-Two's father.

"Isn't it delish?"

"The best I've ever eaten!"

"Have as much as you want. Stuff yourselves, men."

Bulldog Burke watched as beads of sweat broke out on

41

42

the forehead of Jacob Two-Two's father. "Ready to answer our questions now?" he asked, shoving the fragrant platter closer.

"I was ready to answer your questions long ago. After all, Jacob is our son. We all want to find him."

"A likely story. Read him the facts as we know them, Bailey."

"According to our information, you smuggled this deadly dragon into the country out of Kenya. But we are assured by our esteemed colleague, Professor Kilowatt, that he stands two stories high and weighs ten tons. How did you sneak him into the country, man? Come clean."

"I brought Dippy into this country in a cigar box."

"In a cigar box?"

"Yes."

"Take us for fools, do you?"

"I'm telling you the truth."

Turning to the other officers, Bulldog Burke said, "Tell the prime minister this is one tough nut we're stuck with here. But, by George, we'll break him yet, or my name isn't Bulldog Burke. Now, who would like another helping of juicy, tender smoked meat?"

10

Twin posters were banged onto post office walls all across the country. One, featuring a picture of Jacob Two-Two, read:

WANTED
DEAD OR ALIVE
CANADA'S MOST DANGEROUS DESPERADO
JACOB TWO-TWO
$1,000,000 REWARD

Then, at the bottom of the poster, in print so small that you needed a magnifying glass to read it:

Due to a shortage of funds, the government of Canada will pay out this reward at the rate of one dollar a year over a million years.

It was signed:

The Right Honorable Perry Pleaser,
Your lovable, huggable Prime Minister

The other poster, featuring a most unflattering drawing of Dippy, read:

VICIOUS, VILE DRAGON AT LARGE
WANTED BY
PERRY PLEASER, THE DRAGON-SLAYER

Distinguishing characteristics:
He's left-handed and there is a crescent-shaped mole under his right armpit. If in doubt, take his blood pressure. It should read NORMAL.

11

Canada's MOST DANGEROUS DESPERADO and VICIOUS, VILE DRAGON AT LARGE had an absolutely wonderful time their first two weeks on the road. Galloping west, they kept to the wilderness, where they saw deer and moose and bears and beavers and hawks. They passed winding rivers and clear lakes and rushing mountain streams and waterfalls. Jacob Two-Two fished for trout and bass and sometimes for the fearsome northern pickerel. Nobody asked him to wash his hands before dinner or told him what time to go to bed or said that it wasn't good for him to eat a chocolate bar for breakfast. He never had to say things twice, because Dippy listened carefully to everything he said the first time.

The most fun of all was camping together at night under the stars. Jacob Two-Two would set up his tent, gather wood for a fire, and prepare his dinner. Sometimes he would fry a freshly caught fish. Other times he would shop for his food in a neighboring village and then toast hot dogs and marshmallows over the fire until his stomach ached.

Late at night, however, Jacob Two-Two sometimes felt lonely and blue. Happily, it turned out that good old Dippy could sing as fine a baritone as any member of the glee club. Dippy's favorite song, and Jacob Two-Two's, too, was "A Bicycle Built for Two."

As darkness fell, Dippy would wind his huge bulk around the tent to protect it from the wind as well as to keep it warm. Then he would curl his long neck so that he could set his head down alongside the fire. Together they would harmonize, belting out:

> *"Daisy, Daisy, give me your answer, do,*
> *I'm half crazy, all for the love of you.*
> *It won't be a stylish marriage,*
> *I can't afford a carriage,*
> *But you'll look sweet, on the seat,*
> *Of a bicycle built for two."*

Dippy's voice in full flow was very, very loud. When he hit and held a high note, he shattered farm windows three miles away from their camp.

Jacob Two-Two didn't want to complain, but Dippy, in some respects, was an awkward traveling companion. If he was happy and wagged his tail, he could knock down a stand of trees quicker than a team of lumberjacks. If he sneezed, telephone poles would be blown over one mile out of camp. Once, when they had settled down less than a mile outside of Saskatoon, Dippy farted. "Pardon me," he said. But the fact is, he created such a thundering in town that storm warnings went up.

There was an even bigger problem: satisfying Dippy's ten-ton appetite.

For the first few weeks Dippy was content to eat once a day, after dark, chewing his way through a two-acre potato field or an acre of sweet corn. When they moved farther west he would munch through a field of wheat or barley faster than any harvesting machine yet devised by man. He also acquired a taste for apple trees, branches and all, fields of unripe pumpkins, and above all, acres of onions.

As for Jacob Two-Two, he could always slip into a village and buy fresh supplies for himself in a store, but once he found out about the WANTED posters, he realized that he had to be careful. Very careful. Jacob Two-Two first saw the posters pinned to a wall in a convenience store that also served as a post office. When nobody was looking, he pulled the posters free and then took them back to camp to show Dippy.

"What are we going to do now?" Jacob Two-Two asked, frightened.

"Don't ask a prehistoric dunce like me," Dippy said. "You're the brains of this outfit."

Poor outfit, Jacob Two-Two thought.

The truth is, Canada's MOST DANGEROUS DESPER-ADO and VICIOUS, VILE DRAGON AT LARGE were being hotly pursued.

At least once a day a locator airplane wheeled and dipped overhead or a helicopter swooped low over the fields. As soon as they heard an engine in the sky, however,

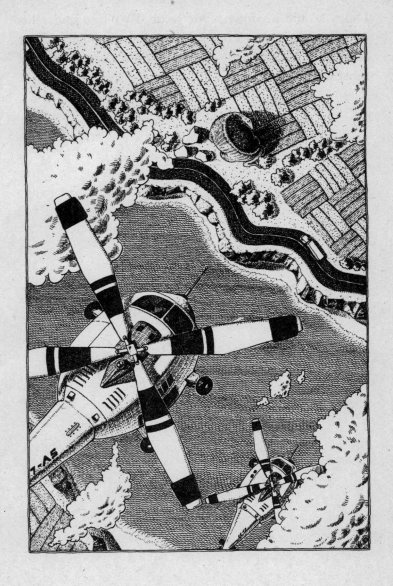

Dippy would lie down, hide Jacob Two-Two under his curling neck, and look for all the world like a huge boulder covered in green moss—or so the most wanted boy and beast in Canada hoped.

12

Meanwhile, there was trouble in the Dragon-Slayer's camp.

"You promised me I was going to be a hero," Perry Pleaser whined.

"Don't worry. They'll be putting up statues in your honor once we catch them," Wacko said.

Yes, said the yes men, and yes, said the yes women, too.

"But what if they escape?" Perry Pleaser asked.

"They can't escape. We're hot on their trail. All we have to do is follow the ruined fields of potatoes and wheat and onions and we're bound to catch up with them. Maybe tomorrow."

But the next morning there was another problem.

"I've been reading up on Saint George," Perry Pleaser said. "If he had a sword, why can't I have one?"

"Attacking as large a dragon as Dippy with a crummy old sword would be about as effective as pricking your finger with a pin," Wacko replied.

Perry Pleaser leaped back from him. "Don't you dare

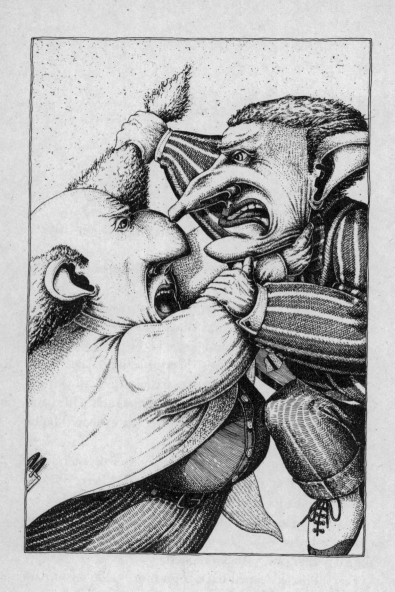

try it, you bully. I have very sensitive skin. And besides, I still think I deserve a sword. So there!"

"Look, Pleaser, Saint George would have given his right arm for the kind of dragon-slaying force you command. Tanks and helicopters and heat-seeking missiles and cannons and bombers. We're going to blast that dippy *Diplodocus* to kingdom come!"

"What if we kill Jacob Two-Two in the attack?"

"Then we'll give him a military funeral. All the trimmings. You'll look just great weeping over him on TV."

Yes, said the yes men, and yes, said the yes women, too.

"Couldn't it make me . . . unpopular?"

"Think again, Pleaser. Do kids have a vote?"

"No, but their parents do. Why, I have two kids myself."

"Yeah, and what good are they? Tell me, Pleaser, if you come home from an exhausting trip, what is the first thing they ask you?"

"Did I bring them a present."

"And if you bundle them into all their winter clothing and boots and scarves, because they just *have* to play in the snow, what happens five minutes later?"

"They want to come in for a pee."

"Let's face it, Pleaser, kids aren't like you or me. They're childish. Why, you put two of them in a room and before you know it they're biting and pinching and scratching each other."

"Weren't you ever a child, Wacko?"

"Yes, but things were different then. I was perfect."

"So was I."

"But I was more perfect than you were," Wacko said, kicking Perry Pleaser in the shin.

"No, you weren't," Pleaser said, kicking him back harder.

"Oh, yes I was too," Wacko said, pinching him.

"Oh, no you weren't," Pleaser insisted, spitting at him.

In an instant they were rolling over and over in the dirt, pinching and scratching and biting. Two generals had to separate them.

"Who started this?" one of the generals asked.

"He did," Perry Pleaser whined between sobs.

"Liar! You did!"

"Sez who, shorty?"

"Sez me, mutton-head!"

"This has got to stop," the general pleaded. "You are setting a bad example for the troops. Save your fire for the dragon, gentlemen."

"Yes," Wacko said. "And that dreadful Jacob Two-Two, too. Because this is war and he will just have to take his chances."

13

Four weeks into their hike to the Rocky Mountains of B.C. there was suddenly no more joy for Jacob Two-Two in eating enough toasted hot dogs and marshmallows to make him feel sick to his stomach. What he really longed for now was his mother's marvelous chili, her incomparable roast chicken, and, he had to admit, her hugs, her kisses, and the stories she read to him before he went to sleep. He also missed horsing around with his father and even the teasing of his two stinky older brothers and two stinky older sisters. His longing led him to take a big risk. He slipped into a small town, found an all-night pizza parlor, and ordered a king-size L'Abbondanza made with tomato sauce, garlic sausage, green peppers, olives, and cheese. Then he took it back to camp to eat. It was too much. He couldn't finish it. So he offered the other half to Dippy, who gobbled it up, smacking his lips. "Hey," he said, "this is terrific stuff! How about fetching me some?"

In spite of the danger, Jacob Two-Two returned to the all-night pizza parlor. "Do you deliver?" he asked.

"Sure, kid, what do you want?"

"Fifty king-size L'Abbondanzas."

"Holy cow! That will come to three hundred and fifty dollars. You'll have to pay cash."

Jacob Two-Two counted out the money and an hour later was out on the road with the delivery man. "Just another mile down the highway," Jacob Two-Two said. "You see that big green boulder? We stop right there."

"Funny," the delivery man said, pulling up, "I've come this way maybe a thousand times, but I've never seen that green boulder before."

"It's always been here," Jacob Two-Two said, alarmed. "It's always been here."

The delivery man unloaded the pizzas. He glanced at the green boulder again and suddenly his hair was standing on end. "My God!" he shouted. "It's moving! That boulder has red eyes! Out of my way, kid!" And he leaped into his truck, made a quick U-turn, and sped away.

"Dippy," Jacob Two-Two said, "you were supposed to sit absolutely still, with your head tucked in."

"I know, I know, but the smell was driving me bananas. I thought he'd never get those pizza pies unloaded."

"Let's get out of here," Jacob Two-Two said.

So they galloped back to camp before Dippy sat down to his feast. "Oh boy, oh boy," he said. "Yum, yum."

One minute there were fifty pizzas on tin-foil plates stacked in rows of ten and the next minute—gobble, gobble, gulp, gulp—there were none. "Say," Dippy said,

smacking his lips, "that was great for starters. Now what's for the main course?"

"What's for the main course? Gimme a break, Dippy."

"I'm still hungry."

"You're always hungry, Dippy."

An hour later Dippy wasn't feeling well. He rolled over on his back, moaning and groaning. "Ooooh," he wailed, "ooooh, what have I done? My poor, aching stomach."

"Well, no wonder. You weren't supposed to eat the tin-foil plates, too, Dippy. That isn't even civilized."

"But I'm not civilized. I'm just a prehistoric slob. Ooooh," he moaned again. "Ooooh, now I understand how my unhappy ancestors disappeared. It wasn't because we were airheads or there was a meteorite shower. There must have been somebody running a prehistoric pizza parlor back in the old swamp. Oooooh me, ooooh my!"

"Stop it, Dippy. You're giving me a pain."

"I'm never going to find a nice girl *Diplodocus* in the Rockies of B.C. I'm going to die right here. A poor, homeless orphan dinosaur. The last of a noble line."

"Why don't you try to walk if off, Dippy?"

Dippy rolled onto his feet, still groaning, and began to walk about in circles, his head hanging low. But he had not yet properly digested the tin-foil plates. Each time he took a step it sounded like a hundred tin cans were being kicked downhill. Jacob Two-Two held his ears. "Dippy, they can hear you miles away. Stop. Sit down."

Dippy sat down. Clunk, clunk, clunk. But the next minute he was burping all over the place, his hot breath uprooting trees and sending them flying. "Oooh," he moaned. "Poor me. Poor little me."

"I'll tell you what," Jacob Two-Two said. "We'll try a song. Maybe that will help take your mind off things."

Together they sang:

> "Daisy (burp, burp), Daisy (belch, belch),
> Give me your answer, do (burp, belch) . . ."

And so on, far into the night.

14

A flood of fascinating information began to pour into the Dragon-Slayer's camp, which lay only four miles away. The information came from Banff, not quite in B.C., but certainly in the Rocky Mountains. A pizza parlor owner called to say a kid who looked just like CANADA'S MOST DANGEROUS DESPERADO had been in earlier for a takeout order of fifty L'Abbondanza pizzas. The man said he wouldn't have served him, but the kid was carrying a machine gun and had twelve hand grenades hanging from his belt. Next, the delivery man explained how, held at gunpoint, he had delivered the pizzas to a remote part of the highway. "There was a big green boulder out there with red eyes," he said.

"Get that cuckoo off the phone," Wacko said, "Scientifically speaking, there is no such thing as a boulder with red eyes."

Then a reporter got on the phone to Bailey to say the town had just been hit by a fierce wind filled with flying trees.

"So Banff's been hit by another windstorm. Big deal."

"Yeah," Bailey said, "but this particular one stinks of garlic sausage, green peppers, olives, and cheese."

"Just like L'Abbondanza pizzas," Perry Pleaser said, licking his lips. "Hey, let's order up some."

Yes, said the yes men, rubbing their stomachs, and yes, said the yes women, rubbing their stomachs, too.

"Wait," Wacko said. "Let me think. Kid like Jacob Two-Two in pizza parlor. Green moving boulder with red eyes. Flying trees. Wind that stinks of garlic sausage. There has to be a connection there somewhere. Let me feed the information into my computer . . ."

Which was when the singing in the distance started.

"Daisy (burp, burp), Daisy (belch, belch),
Give me your answer, do (burp, belch) . . ."

Next thing they knew, the Dragon-Slayer's camp was being bombarded by flying trees.

"Just what I've been waiting for," Wacko said.

"Wh-wh-wh-what do you mean?" Pleaser asked, his knees knocking.

"I've tricked them into revealing their position."

"When do we attack?" a general asked impatiently.

Wacko yanked a twenty-foot-long sheet out of his computer. "We have researched some of the most famous military decisions in history. We know the precise hour the siege of Troy began, the very moment Hannibal started across the Alps, and the exact second Caesar wet his feet in the Rubicon. As a result, we have been able to

come up with the most favorable moment to begin any attack. The moment, gentlemen, that absolutely guarantees victory in the field."

"And when is that?" the generals asked, enormously impressed.

"It is our considered opinion that we should attack somewhere between the first light of dawn and midnight. Why don't we toss a coin?"

"We attack at the first light of dawn," the generals insisted.

"C-c-c-couldn't we wait for the second light?" Perry Pleaser asked.

Y-y-yes, said the yes men, and y-y-yes, said the yes women, too.

"As you wish, but then Canada expects every man to do his duty."

"I-I-I have to go to the toilet right away," Perry Pleaser said.

15

That night it began to rain, which did nothing to improve the spirits of either Dippy or Jacob Two-Two, both of whom were feeling frightened and irritated. So close to their destination, but not safe yet. Far from it. "At least," Jacob Two-Two said, "we haven't far to go. We're almost in B.C."

"You sound like you'll be glad to be rid of me."

"That's not true, but I do miss home . . ."

"My home," Dippy said, "will be in distant mountain ranges not yet ruined by man. There I'll find my mate and raise a *Diplodocus* family. We're caring, family-type creatures, you know."

"Sure, Dippy. Whatever you say."

"So why do they want to hunt me down and pulverize me?"

"Let's face it, some people find you kind of scary."

"Me?" he protested. "I'm a vegetarian. Well, for the most part. I do find garlic sausage yummy. But I'm a law-abiding citizen. In more than sixty-five million years I've never even had a ticket for jaywalking."

"Okay, okay. You're perfect."

"I never said that. But people—bah! You've only been around for three million years or so and you've already made a garbage dump out of the earth. When we were lords of the planet there were no factories belching stinky fumes into the air or spilling nasty chemicals into the rivers and oceans. We kept the earth squeaky clean."

"Yeah, sure. But there were also no airplanes or hospitals or TV or books or baseball or glee clubs. Admit it, Dippy, in all your millions of years on earth you guys didn't even invent the wheel. Or chopped chicken liver."

"Hey, how about another batch of pizza. I'm hungry."

"You're always hungry."

"Look here, Jacob, if you think I'm so dumb or difficult, you can head home right now. I can make it the rest of the way into B.C. myself."

"Oh, yeah," Jacob Two-Two said, his eyes filling with tears, "I bet you'd get lost without me."

"Like heck I would," Dippy said, starting to cry himself.

"I don't want to quarrel. Let's go to sleep, Dippy."

"You need a lot more sleep than I do. I could make better time without you."

"Is that how you really feel?" Jacob Two-Two asked.

"Yes," Dippy said.

"All right, then," Jacob Two-Two said, beginning to pack his things. "I'll leave right now."

65

"See if I care," Dippy said.

But as he watched Jacob Two-Two trudge off into the dark and rainy and thundering night, Dippy was weeping buckets. Good-bye, old friend, he thought. Good-bye and good luck. Maybe someday you'll understand that I knew the enemy was approaching with their tanks and heat-seeking missiles and bombers, and that I couldn't bear to have you around once the final battle began.

16

Stumbling down a hill in the first light of dawn, the straps of his backpack biting into his shoulders, Jacob Two-Two ran into a small figure carrying a white flag and a suitcase. It was Professor Wacko Kilowatt.

"Hi there, Jakey-baby. How good to see you."

"I'll bet," Jacob Two-Two said. "I'll bet."

"We've got to talk fast, kiddo. Perry P. and his dragon-slaying unit are only a couple of hours behind us."

"What's there to talk about? What's there to talk about?"

"I've been worried about you, Jakey."

"Since when did you become so fond of kids?"

"Well, Jakey, kids *are* a nuisance and that's the truth, but there is hope. Scientifically speaking, on average, kids grow one year older every year. In fact, twenty years after they are born all kids become adults and therefore acceptable company. Isn't that wonderful news?"

Jacob Two-Two groaned.

"Look, I brought prezzies and some things for a picnic."

Wacko sat down on the grass and began to pull things out of his suitcase. A stuffed bunny rabbit.

"Oh, no," Jacob Two-Two said.

A jump rope. A Sony Walkman. And, finally, good things to eat. Smoked salmon. Chopped egg sandwiches. Potato chips. Chocolate bars. Jacob Two-Two dug in greedily.

"Incidentally," Wacko asked, as if he had just remembered, "how's your friend Dippy?"

"He's not my friend anymore."

"Hardly surprising. I never trusted him. He has the most dishonest green face I ever saw."

"He threw me out of camp," Jacob Two-Two said.

"Why, that ungrateful dumb dino! After all you did for him!"

"Yes," Jacob Two-Two said, feeling absolutely miserable.

"I'm going to let you in on a secret, kid. It's time Jacob Two-Two and Wacko learned to look after themselves."

"How? How?"

"Do you see any point in blowing up Dippy to kingdom come?"

"No," Jacob Two-Two said in a small voice.

"What we want to do is take the beast alive. Cage the monster! Then we charge people to see him. A genuine *Diplodocus!* A vicious prehistoric beast weighing ten tons, with brains the size of a peanut!"

Poor Dippy, Jacob Two-Two thought.

"Say we attract two thousand suckers a day at five bucks

each. Wait," Wacko said, pulling out his calculator. "That makes seventy thousand dollars a week, less expenses, my manager's fees, and so forth. We could be partners. Share and share alike. How much is your allowance, Jakey-baby?"

"Two dollars a week."

"I'll give you fifty dollars a week. How about that?"

"What do I have to do for all that money?"

"Lead the brute into a cage, that's all. I'll handle everything else." Wacko pulled a contract out of his pocket. "Sign here, kiddo."

"I don't know, Wacko. I don't think Dippy would like being held in a cage."

"It's either being caged by us or pulverized by Perry P. We'd be doing him a favor."

Jacob Two-Two began to sob.

"What's wrong?" Wacko asked.

"You don't know how difficult it's been for me these past few weeks, stuck out in the wilds with a dumb dinosaur. I never had anybody to play with."

"Sign here, partner, and I'll play with you."

"Would you play with me now?"

"Jakey," Wacko said, glancing at his wristwatch, "Perry P. and his army will strike within the hour. We haven't got much time."

"Would you please play with me for only ten minutes?"

"And then you'll sign?"

"Yes."

"What do you want to play?"

"Hide-and-seek. You're it."

"What do I do?"

"Lay your head against that tree, shut your eyes tight, count to a hundred, then come and find me."

"You mustn't go too far. We have to hurry."

"I won't. I won't."

"Okay," Wacko said, leaning against the tree, his head hidden in his arms. "Starting. One. Two. Three. Four . . ."

Jacob Two-Two leaped up, grabbed the jump rope, and wound it around and around Wacko, knotting it tight.

"Hey," Wacko said, "what's going on here?"

"Nobody's going to cage *or* pulverize Dippy. I'm going to find him and lead him to safety in the Rockies of B.C. So long, Wacko."

"Come back, Jacob. Come back at once!"

But Jacob Two-Two was gone.

17

"Dippy! Dippy!"

Jacob Two-Two ran. He ran and ran. He ran all the way back to camp, but he was too late.

Dippy was gone.

"Oh, Dippy," Jacob Two-Two cried, "I didn't mean any of the things I said. I love you."

Obviously, before he had quit the camp, Dippy had suffered a temper tantrum. Uprooted trees were strewn about the fields here, there, and everywhere. Wandering amidst the fallen trees, Jacob Two-Two stumbled on the last things left in the camp where they had once been so happy together. There were the WANTED posters he had brought back from the convenience store that time. The VICIOUS, VILE DRAGON AT LARGE poster was intact, but not the poster saying WANTED, DEAD OR ALIVE, CANADA'S MOST DANGEROUS DESPERADO. Dippy had torn Jacob Two-Two's picture out of that poster. Obviously he had taken it with him.

Oh, my, Jacob Two-Two thought, tears of joy coming

74

to his eyes. I'm forgiven. I'm forgiven. His heart soared. He wanted to cheer. But just then a helicopter swooped out of the sky and landed nearby. Four combat-ready soldiers leaped out of it.

"There's the desperado!"

Even as Jacob Two-Two struggled, howling and kicking, they dumped him into the helicopter and took off again, rising over the trees strewn here, there, and everywhere.

"I don't care," Jacob Two-Two said. "Dippy's safe. You'll never catch him now. Yippee for B.C.!"

Then all at once the helicopter began to rock in the sky. The next mountain peak trembled with explosions. Debris flew into the air. Smoke spiraled into the sky. Then the bombers flew over the peak again, unloading even more of their deadly missiles. The mountain peak shook and trembled once more.

"Well, that's it," a soldier said. "He's been pulverized."

"The dragon is no more!"

"Oh, no," Jacob Two-Two moaned. "Oh, no."

18

Perry Pleaser's face filled the TV screen. "Hurray for me," he said. "I'm now a hero, just like Saint George."

Yes, called out the yes women, standing in the background, and yes, called out the yes men, too.

"You can show how pleased you are by putting up statues of me on the main streets of all your cities. I won't object. You can also compose symphonies in my praise. Or operas, if you prefer. I'm sorry the beast's final death struggle could not be shown on TV, but it was just too, too ghastly. There was blood and gristle everywhere. I mean, boy, did I ever pulverize him! So now, my people, you can sleep easily in your beds. You are safe. Why, I was even able to save that poor, innocent boy the dragon had so cruelly kidnapped. Yes, Jacob Two-Two is home again. With no thought for my personal safety, I charged in and plucked the child from the dragon's claws. Fearless, that's me. Vote for Perry Pleaser, your hero and mine. Thank you very much and now, good night, fans."

19

Jacob Two-Two was certainly pleased to be home again. There was no doubt about that. But he wouldn't eat. He hardly ever spoke. He wasn't sleeping well. He had dark circles under his eyes. And if anybody so much as mentioned Dippy he burst into tears.

Poor pulverized Dippy hadn't meant any harm. All he had wanted was a mate and a quiet life in the Rockies of B.C.

Then, only a week after Jacob Two-Two had come home, Perry Pleaser's victory speech was shown on TV again.

"We can switch to another channel," Jacob Two-Two's mother said anxiously.

"No, I want to see it. I want to see it."

What did Perry Pleaser mean, saying Jacob Two-Two had been kidnapped and that he had rescued him from the dragon's claws? What a fibber. Wow! And why hadn't he shown Dippy's body on TV? I mean, he's such a braggart, that Pleaser. *What if there was no body? What if he was fibbing about that, just as he had lied about rescuing Jacob Two-Two?* No, that was too much to hope for. Dippy's dead.

Poor Dippy.

A month passed, then another month, Jacob Two-Two getting thinner and thinner, his parents grieving. Then one morning there was a very odd item in the newspaper.

Rocky Mountain Mystery
PIZZA PARLOR ROBBERIES IN B.C.

KAMLOOPS, B.C. —Last night somebody broke into a pizza parlor and took off with fifty all-dressed L'Abbondanzas. The cash register was left undisturbed. Nothing else was taken. This was the twentieth such L'Abbondanza robbery in the Rockies over the past two months. Each robbery is followed by a baffling windstorm. The wind, residents claim, reeks of garlic sausage, green peppers, olives, and cheese. Sometimes it is filled with flying trees.

Police are puzzled, but they are continuing with their investigations and promise to capture the pizza parlor pilferers soon.

Two days later there was another disturbing news story out of B.C. Mountain climbers, scaling a peak in the Rockies, had decided to camp for the night on an enormous green boulder. But as they hammered in their tent pegs the boulder had suddenly cried "Ouch!" and then actually shaken off the climbers and tent. Interviewed by reporters, one of the climbers claimed that not only had the boulder moved, but also that it had two large blinking red eyes. But further questioning revealed that this poor climber had fallen on his head.

That very evening there was something even curiouser on the TV news. Paleontologists scaling a hitherto unexplored Rocky Mountain peak had been awakened in the middle of the night by a perfectly appalling noise, seemingly coming from an adjoining peak. Had they not known better, they would have sworn that it sounded like two voices, one male and the other female, harmonizing. In fact, one of the paleontologists claimed that he could make out the words. According to him, they were:

Daisy, Daisy, give me your answer, do,
I'm half crazy, all for the love of you.
It won't be a stylish marriage,
I can't afford a carriage,
But you'll look sweet, on the seat,
Of a bicycle built for two.

Jacob Two-Two, his eyes glued to the TV set, suddenly began to rock with laughter.

"Jacob," his mother exclaimed, delighted, "are you feeling better?"

Everybody raced off to the kitchen to bring Jacob Two-Two his favorite foods.

"Good old Jake," Daniel said.

"Hurray for my little brother," Noah said.

"Am I ever relieved," Emma said.

"Me too," Marfa said.

But there was even more to come on TV the next morning. "Sssh," Jacob Two-Two said, watchful.

Further investigation of the hitherto unexplored Rocky Mountain peak had revealed a huge winding trench dug in a hidden valley. Paleontologists were convinced that this was evidence of an earlier civilization, most likely Indian, maybe fifty thousand years old. It would, however, take them years of research to decipher the coded message of the winding trench, obviously an appeal to ancient gods, composed in a language no longer known to man. For if it was read in English it just didn't make sense. It was gibberish. Then they showed a picture of the winding trench taken from a helicopter. The message looked like this:

Some dinosaur, Jacob Two-Two thought, laughing out loud again. Some dumb dinosaur. "Yippee for Dippy!" he cried out.

ABOUT THE AUTHOR

MORDECAI RICHLER, an eminent Canadian novelist, is the author of several highly acclaimed adult novels—*The Apprenticeship of Duddy Kravitz, Stick Your Neck Out, Cocksure,* and *Joshua Then and Now* among them. His first book for children, *Jacob Two-Two Meets the Hooded Fang*, was hailed as "one of the funniest rampages in all literature," and stars the same irrepressible child champion as does this sequel, *Jacob Two-Two and the Dinosaur.* Mordecai Richler has also written many screenplays (including the film version of his own *Duddy Kravitz*) and was the editor of *The Best of Modern Humor.* He lives in Montreal, Canada, and is the father of five children who have the same names as Jacob and his brothers and sisters in the story.

ABOUT THE ILLUSTRATOR

NORMAN EYOLFSON is a young artist who lives in Toronto, Canada. His work appears regularly as editorial commentary in newspapers and magazines. This is his first book.

The long-awaited sequel to
The Chocolate Touch
is finally here!

When John Midas enters a forbidden cave in the Australian Outback, he stumbles into the beginning of time!

John Midas thinks this Christmas vacation could be his best ever—the Midas family is bound for Australia! But while his family examines ancient cave paintings, John wanders into the forbidden sacred caves of Ayers, and into a very different world. He finds himself in the Dreamtime, the mythical place where time itself began. Here John must use his twentieth-century knowledge to teach the Australian aborigines the most basic survival skills.

JOHN MIDAS IN THE DREAMTIME will be available in November. If you haven't read it yet, you'll want a copy of *The Chocolate Touch*. You can find a copy at your local bookstore or order below:

☐ THE CHOCOLATE TOUCH 15479-6/$2.50

KIDS!
It's Time to Get NUTTY!

☐ NUTTY FOR PRESIDENT
by Dean Hughes   15376-5/$2.50 ($2.95C)

Class clown, Frederick "Nutty" Nutsell and his friends agree: William Bilks is a nurd. But they're in for a big surprise. William is really a genius in disguise, and he is going to prove it by getting Nutty elected the school's first fifth-grade student council president!

☐ NUTTY AND THE CASE OF THE MASTERMIND THIEF
by Dean Hughes   15414-1/$2.50 ($2.95C)

This second *Nutty* book finds Nutty and his friends trying to solve the mystery of who stole the Christmas Fund money from his locker. The school is turned upside down as Nutty and company endeavor to uncover the real—and very surprising—thief!

New! Coming in April!
NUTTY CAN'T MISS
by Dean Hughes

Nutty's father has taken over coaching the school basketball team, and while Mr. Nutsell knows all about school spirit—he knows very little about basketball! Can child genius William Bilks get Nutty out of this one and restore the team's reputation?
On Sale: March 1988.